Weymouth's
TIMEWALK

A 'choose your own direction' journey through Weymouth's dark and charismatic history!

Written and illustrated by Liam R. Findlay
for Weymouth Museum

Weymouth's TIMEWALK is a historical adventure book by Liam R. Findlay for Weymouth Museum, based on the original scripts and archives of the beloved Timewalk attraction (1990-2010).

ISBN: 9798652053680

Publication copyright © by Weymouth Museum 2020
Text and illustration copyright © by Liam R. Findlay 2020
Photograph copyright © by Weymouth Museum, Liam R. Findlay and Caz Young 2020
Concept art copyright © by John Sunderland and Farmer Studios 2020

All rights reserved. No part of this publication may be reproduced, stored in a retrieval system, or transmitted in any form or by any means without the prior written permission of Weymouth Museum, nor be otherwise circulated in any form of binding or cover other than that in which it is published and without a similar condition being imposed on the subsequent purchaser.

www.weymouthmuseum.org.uk

This story will take you on a walk back in time, journeying through the dark, dangerous and charismatic history of Weymouth. From its challenges as the town where Britain's deadly Black Death first arrived, past explosions and war, to its rebirth as a royal resort, brace yourself for stormy sailing!

As you go along, you will be given choices to jump to different pages and try different paths through history. This means that you can read this book more than once, with a new adventure each time!

Prepare to be taken aback!

THE CAT AND THE CLOCK

If it had been his decision, Sebastian would have been full of cookies and fast asleep by now. Instead, he was full of butterflies and alone. Each of his steps bounced off of the walls as he crept through the old brewery, his torchlight causing shadows to flicker about like ghosts.

Sebastian van Reefknot had only recently moved to the town of Weymouth, so he didn't know much about it, other than that it was by the sea and that the locals liked to argue about traffic lights, or maybe it was fairy lights. He was only twelve years old, but he had hoped getting a job might be a way of making new friends, since he had a grand total of zero in Weymouth. It should have been obvious that Night Security Guard was one of the least friendly jobs he could possibly have picked, but he'd gone for it anyway. For some reason, not even adults seemed to have wanted this job. Sebastian was the only person who had turned up for an interview. It was like there was something about the brewery that everyone knew, and they were keeping it from him.

A sudden, distant rumbling echoed from one of the doors across a dark corridor. Sebastian gulped, then took a deep breath of dusty air. He paced towards the door, slowly pushed it open, then lifted his torch to peer inside.

"Is ... is anyone there?" he whispered, although he had planned for it to be a shout. "The brewery is closed. You're not supposed to be here."

Running the torchlight across the walls, he could see that the room was crammed with mysterious objects: moth-bitten flags, thick books, the portrait of some king, telescopes, and barrels. It smelt of old things. Across the room was a ginormous clock. Its ticking was loud, and its hands were just past midnight.

"Hello! What you doing here?" A woman's voice rang from the darkness. Sebastian leapt back.

"Who's there?" he said. Not far from where he stood was a desk. An old man with a lengthy beard was slumped behind it and occasionally let out deep snores. That's what the rumbling noise must have been. Maybe the man had fallen asleep earlier — maybe he worked for Weymouth Museum and had been researching here. A slender, white cat with big, green eyes and a glistening, jewel-encrusted collar pounced onto the desk from the man's lap. But there were no women around. Where had the voice come from?

"If you're going to stay, keep the noise down, or you'll wake Mr Cross," the voice continued. "If you wake him up, he'll be pretty cross, I can tell you."

"Who's speaking? Where are you?" Sebastian said, waving his torch about.

"I suppose I should introduce myself! I'm Ms Paws, the brewery cat. I was here before this place was the Devenish Brewery, and when Nothe Fort was an empty shell of abandoned ghost tunnels!"

"You? You're the one talking?" Sebastian said. "Cats don't talk!" He stared at the animal on the desk, who now sat upright and gazed into his eyes.

"Shh! Mr Cross has been working real hard today, trying to sort out all these old papers for the Museum — trying to cat-alogue 'em, so to speak! You're new here, aren't you? What's your name?"

"I'm Sebastian," Sebastian said. "This must be a strange dream. Too many cookies before bedtime … I hoped getting a job would help me make friends, but a talking cat isn't what I had in mind!"

"I've been making friends in Weymouth for hundreds of years! You see, I've had eight other lives before this one, going right back to the 14th Century. Here, would you like to meet some of them? They'll make you feel right at home…"

Before Sebastian could ask what Ms Paws was talking about, his torch buzzed wildly. Its light went out. He flinched. Ms Paws started to mutter something in the darkness.

"Oh Devenish clock of ages, seen through the glass,
Open your secrets to those who would pass…"

Suddenly, the big clock's face began to glow. Its hands span backwards, slowly first, then faster. Sebastian stepped towards the door to run away, but it slammed shut.

"Tell the date, the place and the deed,

As you take us through history at a magical speed…"

As if the night couldn't get any stranger, the wall behind the clock disappeared and was replaced by a vast emptiness like the night sky. Mysterious chimes of a music box and the tolls of a bell echoed from beyond.

"Oceans of time, oceans of sea,

Weymouth, tell us your history!"

A force pulls Sebastian behind the clock, into the void. He senses something. If you think he should follow the smell of the sea, **go to PAGE 11.** *If you think he should follow the glint of moonlight,* **go to page 17**.

1347: THE CARGO HOLD

PAGE 11

The ground was moving. Only slightly, but it was shifting about under Sebastian's feet. He didn't know how he got there, but he had found himself inside the dim room of a ship. It was wooden and creaky, with barrels, sacks and ropes piled high against the walls. There was a salty musk.

"Ho there! Good day to thee there, my beauty!" In a small hammock, pinned up between two barrels, was a scrawny, ginger cat. His eyes were bright and yellow with tiny pupils, and Sebastian noticed that rats were hanging from his belt. "Wink Wink Roley be the name!"

"Where am I?" Sebastian said, feeling confused and a little bit unwell.

"Haven't you been at sea before, lad? Us Weymouth folk have been fishing since the Romans came by in ancient times!" Wink said.

"I'm not really at sea though, am I? How do I get back to the clock? Where's Ms Paws? Where's the brewery? What's the date?"

"You sea sick, lad? It be midnight, June, 1347! This vessel's taking Portland wool over to France, then we're coming back with barrels of wine!" Over the edge of his hammock, Wink revealed a hook with a piece of cheese pierced on the end. "For now, I'm dealing with unpaid passengers. You know. The squeaky stowaways."

Something scurried over Sebastian's feet, and he writhed with discomfort. A rat, almost the size of a cat itself, went to nibble on some rope. Wink sprang out of the hammock with a deafening squeal and landed inside a barrel, his scrawny, striped tail swaying from out of the top. His eyes peered out of two holes in the wood.

"These ships' vermin have unloaded a devil's cargo of their own," he said. "*Fleas* that carry *disease* that drops a country to its *knees!*"

"Disease?" Sebastian said. Unnerved and eager to get back to the brewery, he hurried away from the deranged animal, towards a hatch at the end of the cargo hold. Hopefully, it would lead somewhere nicer than the dingy, rat-infested den.

Sebastian sniffs a stench coming from beyond the hatch. If you think he should follow it, **go to PAGE 17**. *If you think Sebastian should find a safer route, go to* **PAGE 27**.

1348: THE BLACK DEATH

PAGE 17

It only took a blink for Sebastian to appear somewhere completely different to where he had just been standing. He was on land, and it was still nighttime, but it didn't feel like it was the same night he had been living through a few seconds ago. His feet pressed into the wet mud of an old-fashioned street — not old-fashioned like his grandmother's pink and brown living room, but old-fashioned in the way that King Arthur might come marching around the corner at any moment.

On the other hand, maybe not. This was no place for a king.

Noxious vapours stung the insides of Sebastian's nose, scratching at his throat and making him cough. Wishing he could work out what was going on, he approached one of the buildings to see if anyone was around. From behind a wooden front door, a man could be heard talking in a sad, lyrical tone.

There was a slit in the door that Sebastian found to peer through, careful not to lean too hard and burst into the building. His eyes had to adjust to the light, which came from a lone, sorry-looking candle. The candle was not the sorriest sight in the room, however. Nor were the grimy walls or the uncomfortable-looking ground, covered by straw. The sorriest sight was the people.

A mother stood beside her little boy, both dressed in Medieval outfits, both gazing down at a man who had been laid upon a wooden bed. He was still. A hooded priest, with robes which reached the ground, was chanting words from a small book, in a language Sebastian hadn't heard before.

"Black cats bring luck, so they say, but today, black is not a lucky colour." Brushing past Sebastian's legs was a solemn cat, as black as the sky. She was another who could talk — one of Ms Paws' so-called nine lives, perhaps. The cat continued with a croaking voice: "Mrs Cornick here, she had a soft heart for an ageing cat like me, but another mouth she can ill afford to feed since her husband has fallen victim to the plague."

"The plague? The Black Death? I've learnt about that at school! Didn't it kill over half of Britain?" Sebastian said. "This isn't the same one, surely? Time travel doesn't exist!"

"Some say that the plague was brought to our shores by a seaman who arrived in Weymouth from France…" the black cat said, before she disappeared into the shadows. Sebastian's heart tremored at the thought of being left alone in the diseased streets. He sped away to find where the cat had gone.

Sebastian hears the cries "bring out yer dead!" from somewhere nearby. To find where the cries are coming from, **continue to the next page**. *To get far away from the Black Death,* **go to PAGE 27**.

1349: THE PLAGUE CART

"Bring out yer dead! Bring out yer dead!"

Two men emerged into the moonlight, their faces hidden behind rags. One pushed and one pulled on a creaky cart, which bounced and squelched over the sodden ground.

Upon the cart was a body.

Sebastian must have stepped into a new time period again, because the body belonged to the priest he had seen standing and chanting in the house, only a moment before. The priest's face was now lifeless, blue and staring blankly.

It was a sight Sebastian would never forget.

"We live under the black shadow of death," the black cat said, emerging from behind the cart. "I hear over a third of Europe's people are likely to be killed. Entire villages such as Came and Witcombe, just outside Weymouth town, have been wiped out. Rich and poor, young and old. It spares no-one."

"I'm sorry..." Sebastian said. Even though he had known a bit about the Black Death, he hadn't known that Weymouth, the town he only recently moved to, was where the disease first arrived.

"Move on quick, boy, before the death cart carries you away!" the black cat said.

"Stay safe, black cat!" Sebastian said, and he ran off.

*Sebastian finds two buildings with their doors open, where he could hide from the terrifying plague cart. If you think Sebastian should explore the building with ropes and fabrics inside, **go to PAGE 27**. If you think Sebastian should explore the building with clatters and bangs inside, **go to PAGE 43**.*

1588: THE SAILMAKER'S LOFT

PAGE 27

"I've walked into another year, haven't I?" Sebastian said, scratching his head. The cat at the top of the stairs looked down at him and raised its brow.

"Shifty's the name," the cat, apparently known as Shifty, said. He was stood, leaning against a crate of silk, with a club in one hand. Around his upper legs were puffy breeches of red and green, and his hair was wild, riddled with black, white and orange tufts. "It's 1588, matey! Friendly place, Weymouth, don't you think?" He swung the club down on the crate, just missing a rat as it poked its head out from under some crumpled fabric.

"Friendly? I'd be glad to run away and never come back!" Sebastian said. He climbed to the top of the steps to sit near Shifty. Around the corner, a long-haired man was sat on a stool, sewing a giant piece of fabric that was draped over his lap.

"My master is completing a top sail for ninety tonnes of English oak and cannon—"

"You mean a ship?" Sebastian asked.

"No, I mean a donkey. Of course I mean a ship! It's going West to teach the Spaniards a thing or two. Armada, Armada ... that's all you hear! There's talk of a thousand Spanish ships sailing towards us as I speak."

"Are we at war with Spain? You just said Weymouth is a friendly place!"

"They've been having some nasty quarrels with Queen Elizabeth. As it happens, my master was told the Spanish Armada was last sighted off of Portland Bill, not far from here! If I were you, I'd be off, lest you lose your head to a cannonball!" Shifty said.

Sebastian rolled his eyes. "I told you I need to get out of this town!"

*If you think Sebastian should ask for help from a family down the road, **go to page 43**. If you think Sebastian should run towards the attack of Spanish Armada, **continue to PAGE 33**!*

1588: THE SAN SALVADOR

PAGE 33

Whatever supernatural forces were playing with Sebastian had thrust him onto one of the Spanish Armada ships that Shifty had described. The reason he knew that the ship was Spanish was because of the accent of the grey cat who decided to scream at him.

"What is this Engleesh heretic pig doing aboard my ship? Huh!" the cat said. He had a pointy beard of fur, a cape, a feathered hat and a cane that he waved above his head.

"Who are you?" Sebastian said, dodging to avoid being hit in the face.

"I am José Cortez, cabin cat of the famous Spanish galleon, the San Salvador! I am guarding the Spanish imperial gold that will finance the invasion of your country!" Sure enough, José was stood on a wide, black treasure chest. Sebastian thought he might have spotted the same chest when he'd been at the brewery before, doing his Night Security Guard rounds through Weymouth Museum. Behind José was a window to the stormy sea, rocking side-to-side, up-and-down. José was clearly well-practiced at keeping his balance. "We are going to destroy your ships and make England part of our great Spanish Empire!"

Without warning, José swung his cane in Sebastian's direction. Sebastian ducked but fell to the ground. While his target was down, José screeched, dropped the cane and drew his claws. He leaped onto Sebastian's arm, causing a sharp pain, digging in deep.

"Ouch!" Sebastian said, struggling to pull the

frenzied cat away.

"With God on our side, we sail to battle and victory!" José drew a sword from under his cape, then pointed it over Sebastian. "Prepare to—"

Every timber around the two of them rattled and cracked. The glass in the window shattered, letting waves crash through the gaps and splatter over Sebastian's legs. By the sound of it, an explosion had smashed through the San Salvador.

"What on earth is happening?" José said in a high-pitched scream, now drenched and shivering. Sebastian wasn't going to hang around much longer. He hurried into a long room, lined with cannons, but many were overturned. Water was rushing in through gigantic holes, and men were strewn around without a sign of life. José pounced left and right, taking in the damage. "Oh no! This is horrible! The explosion has wrecked my beautiful ship! The destruction is terrible! And the crew — just look!

Ahhhhh!" He sprinted wildly up a set of steps.

1588: Looting The San Salvador

Sebastian hurried after José, but when he got to the upper gun deck, all was quiet, and the chaos was gone.

"Have I taken another leap through time?" he said to himself, stepping over a fallen mast and piles of ash.

"I see you've come for some lively looting too!" a familiar voice called. Across the deck was Shifty, the colourful sailmaker's cat, sat upon a chest that was being carried by his master and a struggling apprentice boy.

"What happened here? Where are the crew?" Sebastian said.

Shifty climbed off of the chest and approached with a smug stride. "No one knows what happened," he said. "But it looks like a spark must have lit some of the San Salvador's gun powder. They say she was carrying most of the gun powder for the Spanish fleet. The explosion was heard over six miles away, right down to

Abbotsbury!"

"I was attacked by a cat called José. He drew his sword on me! What happened to him?"

"The explosion killed over two-hundred men, and as for José Cortez, he's rotting away in Weymouth Dungeon, along with the rest of the wretched crew! At the Battle of Portland today, the Spanish fleet were no match for our fast and nimble ships. We towed the San Salvador into Weymouth Bay, and as you can see, we've been collecting a few souvenirs. I'll be glad to get ashore, away from the unbearable stench of dead bodies and the smells of war. As for you, you'd best be on your way, before we take a liking to the trinkets you're wearing!"

Sebastian clasped his hand around the watch on his wrist. He realised that it had stopped ticking. It was probably as confused about all this time travel as he was. Then, as if it could read his mind, the hands began to move again. In fact, they were spinning, and the sound of a music box could he heard in the air. Sebastian knew that he would soon be dropped into the middle of some other ghastly trouble from Weymouth's past.

*If you would like to send Sebastian to the Isle of Portland, Weymouth's neighbour, **go to PAGE 49**. If you would like to send Sebastian somewhere a lot nicer than what he's already had to face, go to **page 65**.*

1643: CIVIL WAR

PAGE 43

Sebastian entered a loud family home, but it wasn't one of celebration, nor did it belong in the same time period as the one he had just been in. This was becoming very dizzying. He quickly hid behind a table, because across the room, a brutish, sword-wielding man seemed to have broken in. A father confronted the intruder, while a horrified wife and crying daughter stood just behind.

"Thank the Lord that ye are come, and brave to be here in this year of our Lord, 1643!" A black-and-white cat with blue eyes poked his head out of a bucket beside Sebastian. "It is fine for a rich merchant's cat like me, Marmaduke Dance, but not safe for any *person* to be in the streets of Weymouth."

"Who is that man?" Sebastian asked. "Is he a pirate?"

"A Royalist vagabond, in full rampant violence!"

"What's a Royalist?"

"He's a man of the King!"

The long-haired, short-tempered Royalist intruder swiped his sword at the father of the house, but the father lifted a stool to stop the blow. The daughter, face full of tears, took a metal plate and threatened to whack the Royalist. Sebastian wanted to help, but Marmaduke asked him a favour:

"Listen! Take note with you out of town to warn others of the barbarism committed by the King's soldiers! 'Tis now two months since the Royalist Earl of Carnarvon entered Dorset with a stout army. When us

Parliamentarians surrendered, the Earl preached that the townsfolk would not be ill-treated, robbed or maliciously victimised. But just see what they do!"

Sebastian nodded and braced himself to run out of the door.

"They will show this family no mercy, and they will pillage this house for valuables," Marmaduke continued. "If they leave the child, if she could only hide, I would go to comfort her, but I fear the worst … When will be the end to this unholy civil war?"

The Royalist intruder had overpowered the cowering Parliamentarian family, and he looked like he was about to do something terrible to them. In a burst of panic, Sebastian picked up a jug from the table and tossed it at the back of the Royalist's head. Now drenched in milk, the villain roared and turned with furious, bulging eyes. Sebastian had already scarpered. When the Royalist ran outside to find who had soaked him, the family slammed their door shut behind.

*If you think Sebastian should warn those by the sea, **go to PAGE 55**. If you think Sebastian should try to find someone in charge, **go to page 65**.*

1675: REBUILDING ST PAUL'S CATHEDRAL

PAGE 49

Sebastian coughed and squinted through clouds of white chalk. All he could make out was rubble, coarse shrubs and blinding sunlight. When he cleared his eyes, he noticed a deep pit of white rock, not far from where he stood. The *plink plink* of hammering rang from somewhere at the bottom.

"Oh, it does make me mad!" A figure stood in the distance, talking to himself. He was short but stood as if he were the tallest person in the world. When Sebastian neared, he could see that the voice belonged to another cat, this one dressed in frills and wearing a bow on his tail. Despite his finery, his jacket was stained with grains of stony dust, and he held a handkerchief over his mouth. "Another claw broken, and why? I'll tell you why: because I have to tramp around this brutal, hard Portland limestone all day, and not a manicure in sight!"

"You think that's bad?" Sebastian said. "People around here have been through a lot worse than a lack of manicures! I've just seen it first-hand!"

The cat rolled his eyes. They seemed fixed at being half-open, casual and condescending. Sebastian couldn't imagine that they'd ever opened any wider. Too much effort, probably.

"'Go and catch a birdie,' says my darling master Christopher," the cat said. "Catch a birdie! Perrywinkle Lydd, a London courtier pussycat, belonging to the rightfully famous architect Sir Christopher Wren, does not 'catch birdies'! Upon my purrfect word, it's enough to give you furballs for a fortnight!"

Sebastian was about to walk away in frustration, when Perrywinkle pulled a big roll of paper from under his jacket. He flicked his wrist, and the document unravelled, revealing a grand sketch of a very well-known building, St Paul's Cathedral.

"Now, don't get me wrong. I don't blame my master Christopher. After all, he was commissioned by Kind Charles II to make good our fair city of London, after the Great Fire. Oh! The heat and all that soot. As I said to my blue Burmese companion at the time, 'Aubrey', I said, 'I like to curl up to a warm fire myself, but this is flipping ridiculous!'"

After all that he had seen, it was easy for Sebastian to forget that other parts of the country had been through challenging histories too. "So Christopher Wren is using Portland stone to help rebuild London?" he said.

"Yes, and just take a look at those peasants cutting the stone. It's not all going to be done by Wednesday week, by any stretch of the imagination. These local types don't deserve Christopher as their Member of Parliament. They accuse of him one minute of commissioning their land for quarrying without compensation, and the next minute, they want him because of his fame to be their MP…" The cat closed his eyes and held his nose high, reeling off his complaints.

Sebastian crept away.

If you think Sebastian should find somewhere full of daring and adventure, **continue to the next page**. *If you think Sebastian deserves an ice cream,* **go to PAGE 73**.

1793: SMUGGLERS

PAGE 55

Like the last biscuit in the tin that you thought was safe from your family, or like his marbles, he supposed, Sebastian was lost again. He ventured into a rocky cavern by the sea shore, hoping he could rest there safely, but in its depths, an ominous glow came into view. Approaching, it appeared that the light was coming from various lanterns, and they were sat upon a mess of wet barrels.

Between the barrels stood a cat, dressed in rugged regalia and leaning against a crutch to support where one of his legs was missing. On his shoulder was a small bird, and over his eye was a patch.

Something didn't feel right about this place. Why was it so hidden away? Who was using it at nighttime? Staying hidden, Sebastian got closer to the animal for a better look.

"Now my beauty, you've got to keep your head low, in case the revenue men get sight of you! We don't want them rumbling what we're up to," the cat warned, startling Sebastian, who didn't think he'd been noticed. "It'll be death by hanging if they catch up with us."

"I'm not part of your ... I'm not up to..." Sebastian mumbled, but then he realised it might be safest to pretend he knew what was going on. "I mean ... aye aye, captain!"

"Dartington O'Keefe's my name, lookout cat and swag runner for Redbeard O'Keefe and his merry band, master smugglers. Are you here to help smuggle this lot?" Dartington said. "Brandy, rum, and over there is tobacco, spices and silk."

Sebastian nodded anxiously, looking around at the containers. He picked up a barrel, so he could pretend he knew what he was doing. It was heavier than he expected — so heavy that he could barely heave it an inch off the ground. Dartington didn't seem to pay any attention, lifting a pipe to his mouth and gazing out towards the cavern entrance, where the moonlight sparkled upon the sea.

"My master and the likes of Isaac Gulliver, the gentleman smuggler, together with that lot from Moonfleet and the murderous gang from Poole … they do enjoy the run of this coast. In the middle of the night, we bring all sorts of goods across the channel from France, on our innocent little boats. We even smuggle people fleeing the revolution … well, them that can afford it! And you won't believe this one: we deliver the King's royal spies to the French shore. Ask no questions. That's the rule. Dead men don't tell tales."

Sebastian swallowed a thick gulp of nervousness. Giving up on the heavy barrel, he lifted a smaller box.

"Hear the hoots outside?" Dartington said. "They're the owlers, hooting down the shore to their men, giving them the all-clear. Time for me to go and lend a hand, then I'll meet with you back in town. You'd better hurry ahead. I'll see you there … But you won't see me!"

Dartington darted outside, so Sebastian put the box down and followed after him. On the shore were men, rolling barrels across the crunching pebbles. A boy with shiny, alert eyes stood upon a lerret boat, grasping a sword by his side. He watched Sebastian hurry towards the town.

When he was among buildings again, Sebastian noticed all sorts of figures sneaking about in the dark. He wasn't sure where he was supposed to meet Dartington, but Dartington had no trouble finding him.

"See the good people of Weymouth?" Dartington whispered from the shadows. Sebastian couldn't see him. "You wouldn't believe they'd be dirtying their hands on smuggled contraband, would you? But now in 1793, so many things have been taxed, it's the only way people can make a living." An older man and his son carried boxes across the street to their home, glancing about with sneers. "See there, Jacob Makepeace and his boy. Them butchers by day. They'll be taking home some sweeter meats tonight: fine cloth, lace, silks and a keg of rum."

A roar of laughter erupted from within one of the other buildings. Sebastian tripped backwards, startled. Through a window was the lively silhouette of a man in a curled wig, waving a glass of drink to and fro.

"Well, if it ain't his eloquence Squire Sedgmoor, magistrate of this town," Dartington's voice continued from its unseen spot. "Tonight, he's holding a party for the local Dorset gentry, and yet, there he is decanting a fine brandy that's not been two days out of our cave. Now, I wonder how he came by that." Although he couldn't see Dartington, Sebastian could hear his wooden leg hitting the cobbles as he walked away. "You'll be safer if you keep heading South than on the shore. I've got better things to do than sit around, watching these folk all night. A lady cat awaits for me, so I'll take my leave. Keep an eye out for the revenue men."

Sebastian didn't know where to nod, so he nodded at the nearest shadow, then he made his way South, where he thought the brewery might be. Or, at least, where it might be in the future.

***Go to page 79** if you'd like to help Sebastian return to the brewery.*

1805: KING GEORGE III

PAGE 65

A fine building on the seafront welcomed Sebastian into its assembly room, where grand music was being played. Gentlemen and ladies, whose faces and hair were so white that they looked like ghouls, danced gracefully, bowed and made polite conversation. Even if they pretended not to, everyone seemed to have their eyes on one man in particular: a pink-faced fellow in a red jacket.

Sebastian stood at the edge of the room, where a cat, dressed in a maid's outfit, was dusting a portrait of the same pink-faced man.

"Don't they all look lovely?" she said. "Just look at his Royal Highness, there in the ruby velvets."

"His Royal Highness? He's the King?" Sebastian said, leaving his mouth open after the end of his question.

"I always come along to the assembly rooms when King George is in Weymouth. I like to spy on the royal party doing their dancing, with its tight patterns and rules of etiquette. Not much like our country dancing. Oh! I forgot to introduce myself! I'm Matilda Tibbs," Matilda Tibbs said.

"I'm Sebastian van Reefknot," Sebastian van Reefknot said. "What's the King doing somewhere like Weymouth? It hardly seems like a relaxing retreat!"

"He first came to Weymouth in 1798. It was his younger brother, William the Duke of Gloucester, who introduced him. He built the royal lodge on the esplanade. The royal party comes here to bathe in the sea, since physicians and fashionable gentlemen say it's good for you. Even drinking it! They drink a pint before breakfast, and sometimes for a change, they have it with crabs' eyes, cuttlefish bones, snails and woodlice."

Sebastian winced. "People are always thinking about their health these days. Or ... those days. Whatever *days* it is now."

"I don't tell many people this, but the King has called me into his library once or twice, sat me on his lap and told me some troublesome things ... about losing the American colonies, and the uprising in France that's seen King Louis and Queen Marie Antoinette lose their heads to the guillotine ... but there I go chattering again!"

Sebastian heard a band playing outside, and when he went to look, it seemed he had taken another trip through time. The ball was now long over, it was daytime, and a crowd was gathered by the sea. The King, wearing only some kind of royal nappy, was climbing out from what appeared to be a white shed on wheels. Someone mentioned that it was a "bathing machine", although it wasn't like any machine Sebastian had used before. It had been positioned in the water so that the King had easy access to dip in and out, with help from a servant. This man must have been Weymouth's first tourist attraction, and judging by their cheers, the locals seemed to love him.

Sebastian strolls along the beach, admiring how Weymouth has broken through its challenges and become such a pleasant and attractive place to be. If you think Sebastian should stay by the beach a while longer, **go to PAGE 73**. *If you think Sebastian should head back to where the brewery might be,* **go to page 79**.

1990: SUMMER HOLIDAYS

PAGE 73

The sun finally began to shine as Sebastian came into a much more familiar time period, although the people were dressed a little bit strangely. Many had their hair greased into flaps that hung to the left and right of their heads like curtains, one woman was wearing dungarees like a miner, and a boy making a sandcastle on the nearby sand had spiky hair with tips that were pale yellow, like they'd been dipped in toilet cleaner. Electric lights lined the esplanade (fairy lights, specifically), tourists paddled, pedalos peddled and donkeys pooed.

Sebastian passed a grand clock tower with Queen Victoria painted in gold on its sides. Sand blew into his face, forcing him to squint. Victoria didn't blink. When he strolled onto the beach, he found a tall, vibrant box with an open window in the front.

"A Punch and Judy show!" Sebastian said, sitting down in front of it, enjoying the warmth around him and the lingering scent of fresh chips.

"Oh hi! What a chance meeting!" A cat popped its head out of the box, and at this point, Sebastian had almost expected it to happen. The cat was a ginger, with sunglasses and a straw hat. "My name's Billy Chance. Round here, they call me Lucky, and I am lucky to be living here in Weymouth. What a lovely place!"

"I wasn't so keen on it at first," Sebastian said. "But I've gotten to know it better this evening. Or this afternoon, I guess. Or over the last few years … or decades … I mean centuries!" He shrugged. "Still, for all the time I've been exploring Weymouth, I still haven't made a single friend."

"There's no limit on the number of friends you could make on a day like today! Weymouth's been a seaside resort since the 18th Century. Oh yes, very fashionable, very friendly. Before King George III made us famous, all the houses faced away from the sea, so we turned them around and built along the esplanade, all elegant like!"

"It sounds like it was a lot fancier than it is today," Sebastian said, looking at the different types of people, old and young, rich and not, who played by the water.

"Weymouth was everything your rich and noble wanted, then in 1857, someone shouted 'all change', just like they do on the railways! That's what happened. The railway reached Weymouth, and *bingo,* all the people in the big cities and towns could reach us for the very first time. The Industrial Revolution gave people a lot more money for their holidays, and they all wanted to spend their pennies and shillings on different thrills and pastimes. Today, the place is more popular than it's ever been, and the people come in their tens of thousands for the same reasons King George III did all those years ago — eh up, Mr Randell's coming back from the betting shop. Time to scarper. See you, and stay lucky. I will!"

An angry-looking man had spotted Lucky Chance and was marching towards the Punch and Judy box. Sebastian stumbled to his feet and hurried into the crowds, finding a sign that would show him the way back to the brewery.

To get Sebastian back where he started, **continue to the next page.**

WEYMOUTH

PAGE 79

The brewery doors were locked when he arrived, but Sebastian still had the keys with him. When he got to the room with the big clock, Ms Paws and Mr Cross had left, and all the papers had been cleared off of the desk. Still, Sebastian knew he was probably back in his own time period, because he'd noticed a familiar poster for Weymouth Museum on his way up, inviting people to join as volunteers. It was a poster he'd seen when he first arrived for his Night Security Guard shift. Left behind on the desk's chair was a modern copy of the local newspaper, and sure enough, it was the date Sebastian hoped it would be. He had returned.

The clock had struck nine, and outside, people could be heard going about their busy business. Sebastian went to join them, standing in the morning sunshine, and he was sure to lock the brewery doors behind him. On the building were big letters, spelling its name: Brewers Quay.

The harbour was lively with tourists and locals, healthy and happy. No sickness, no violence. Those driving the boats looked relaxed as they bobbed along, and Sebastian doubted it was because they had just looted a Spanish galleon or were smuggling barrels of rum from France. At the other end of town, he came across the statue of a regal, pink-faced man.

In front of the statue, near what looked like an old, white shed on wheels, Sebastian found a spot of grass to rest on. When he looked towards the statue again, there was a cat laid by its feet. She was white and wore a jewel-encrusted collar.

"Ms Paws?" Sebastian said, but the cat didn't answer. Cat's don't speak, of course. Still, the familiar sight gave him an unexpected feeling of comfort. He knew the town around him a lot better than he had a few hours before. Perhaps even better than some of the people who had lived there for decades.

Although Sebastian had no friends yet in Weymouth, the town was certainly no stranger to him, and that made him smile.

The cat had disappeared, as cats often do. When Sebastian got up to find her, he discovered her padding up the high-street. Could Mr Cross be wondering where the brewery cat had gotten to? Mr Cross ... The image of the poster Sebastian had seen earlier flashed back into his mind. Weymouth Museum were looking for volunteers, and they probably needed people with a good knowledge of the town's history. He had no friends yet in Weymouth, but Sebastian was sure this wouldn't be the case for much longer.

The end

NOTES FROM THE AUTHOR

My name is Liam, and I have lived in Weymouth all of my life (unlike with Ms Paws, this is the first of my lives). The story you have just experienced is based on a real historical attraction that used to be at Brewers Quay, called The Timewalk.

Much like in this book's story, visitors to The Timewalk would venture through dark, theatrical settings that threw them into Weymouth's lively past. Starting in the brewery office, with an animatronic Ms Paws and a snoring Mr Cross, the wall behind a mysterious clock would draw back to reveal a hidden path.

Sunderland   THE DEVENISH BREWERY   "THE 'OLD MAN OF WEYMOUTH' IN THE NEWSROOM/BOOK ARCADE — WITH 'TAVIS' HIS CAT."

This would happen as Ms Paws recited her magic words to the sound of a Victorian music box and a bell toll. Walking past where the wall had just been, visitors would find themselves in life-like and immersive sets, with dramatic lighting, sound effects and a host of cat characters to explain what was going on! You may have noticed photographs of these scenes throughout this book.

The Timewalk opened in 1990, project-directed by Roger Dalton, who was in charge of transforming the old Devenish brewery into Brewers Quay, a fabulous, rustic shopping centre and museum space. He had hired John Sunderland to develop The Timewalk's concept, John being a pioneer in the idea of "museums being more like movies" in the 1980s. The famous JORVIK Viking Centre, an authentically-constructed, smelly, noisy Viking village experience, was a project of John's, and he applied his skills to The Timewalk in a similar way. The attraction was an instant success, and becoming such a profound part of the town, it earned respect as a significant piece of Weymouth's history in its own right. I hope that this book helps to preserve some of the magic that it offered.

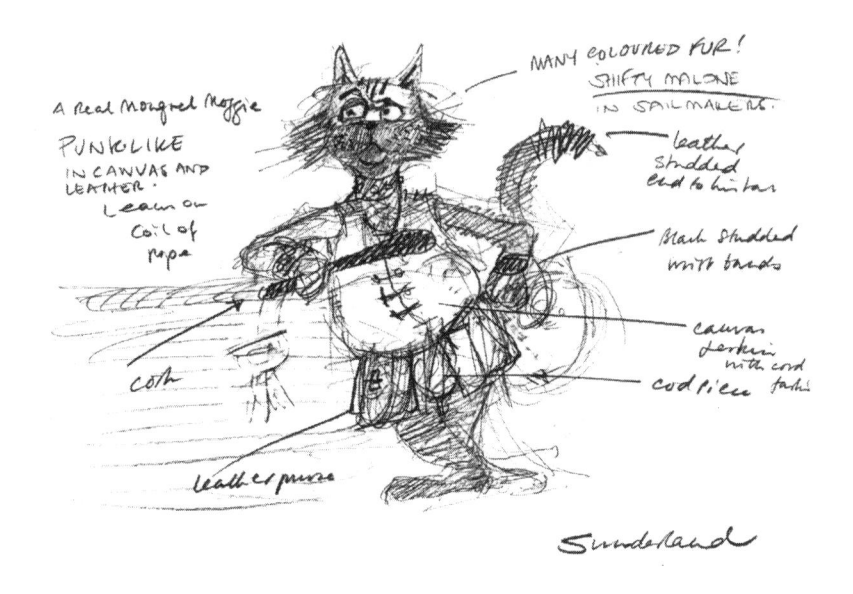

A Real Mongrel Moggie — PUNK-LIKE IN CANVAS AND LEATHER. Lean on coil of rope

MANY COLOURED FUR! SHIFTY MALONE IN SAILMAKERS.

leather studded end to his bar

Black studded wrist bands

canvas jerkin with cord

codpiece fashi...

cosh

leather purse

Sunderland

Many past visitors to The Timewalk remember its unusual smells most of all, as smell has such a powerful connection to our memories and emotions! There was a musty smell in Mr Cross' office, and people recall the stench of the Black Death scenes too. Having grown up to become an attractions designer myself, I now work for

AromaPrime, the company who created The Timewalk's memorable pongs. In an effort to bring some fun, fond memories back to past visitors, I decided to release the original Timewalk scent on AromaPrime's website, aromaprime.com!

The Timewalk sadly had to close in 2010, and I was quick to rescue the Civil War human characters and a smuggler boy, who now live at my home! Later, in 2018, I completed a research project to document The Timewalk's full history, which is on my website,

The Art of Themed Attractions. To gather information and images, I was granted access to Weymouth Museum's archives, where they have kept original designs, scripts and promotional material. I later used these artefacts to help me write and illustrate this book in a way that was authentic to the original attraction experience.

Although The Timewalk closed, we are still very lucky to explore Weymouth's history through Weymouth Museum. Its hard-working team enable us to access all sorts of amazing pieces of the town's past, and it is important that we continue to support it as much as we can. I hope that the sale of this book contributes towards that.

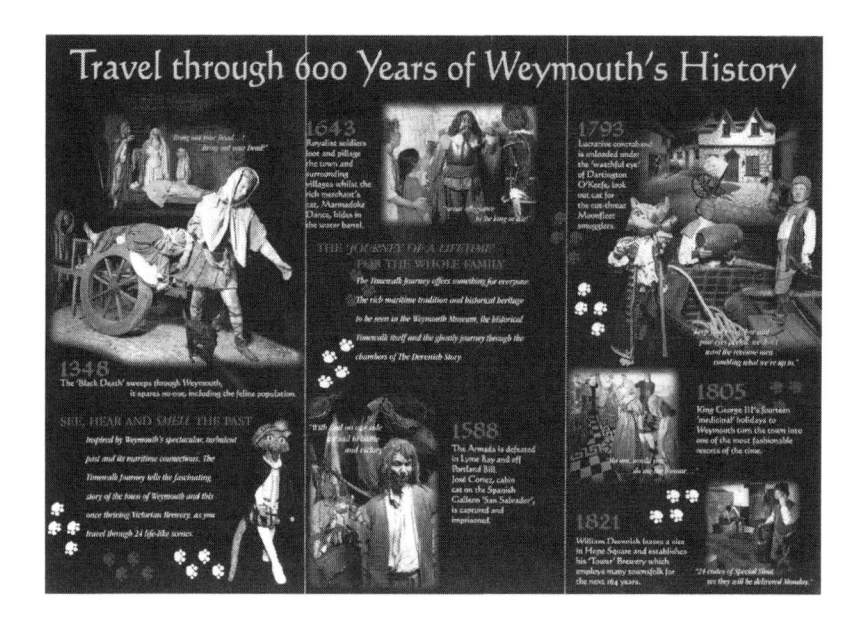

Please enjoy many journeys through time with this book and with Weymouth Museum!

Liam R. Findlay

@Pevalwen

Printed in Great Britain
by Amazon